W9-AAY-728

# Dear Parent:
## Your child's love of reading starts here!

Every child learns to read in a different way and at his or her own speed. Some go back and forth between reading levels and read favorite books again and again. Others read through each level in order. You can help your young reader improve and become more confident by encouraging his or her own interests and abilities. From books your child reads with you to the first books he or she reads alone, there are I Can Read Books for every stage of reading:

### SHARED READING
Basic language, word repetition, and whimsical illustrations, ideal for sharing with your emergent reader

### BEGINNING READING
Short sentences, familiar words, and simple concepts for children eager to read on their own

### READING WITH HELP
Engaging stories, longer sentences, and language play for developing readers

### READING ALONE
Complex plots, challenging vocabulary, and high-interest topics for the independent reader

### ADVANCED READING
Short paragraphs, chapters, and exciting themes for the perfect bridge to chapter books

**I Can Read Books** have introduced children to the joy of reading since 1957. Featuring award-winning authors and illustrators and a fabulous cast of beloved characters, I Can Read Books set the standard for beginning readers.

A lifetime of discovery begins with the magical words **"I Can Read!"**

*Visit www.icanread.com for information*
*on enriching your child's reading experience.*

I Can Read Book® is a trademark of HarperCollins Publishers.

Mia Sets the Stage
Copyright © 2013 by HarperCollins Publishers
All rights reserved. Manufactured in China.
www.icanread.com
Book design by Sean Boggs
Library of Congress catalog card number: 2012944109
ISBN 978-0-06-208686-0 (trade bdg.) —ISBN 978-0-06-208685-3 (pbk.)
Book design by Sean Boggs
12 13 14 15 16   SCP   10 9 8 7 6 5 4 3 2 1
❖
First Edition

# I Can Read!

SHARED
My
First
READING

# Mia
## Sets the Stage

## by Robin Farley
### pictures by Aleksey and Olga Ivanov

HARPER
An Imprint of HarperCollinsPublishers

The big recital
is next week.

Mia and her friends
are very busy.

The dancers pick out costumes.

7

# The dancers plan the set.

# Miss Bird plans the dance.

# The dancers practice.

"The show
will be great!"
sings Miss Bird.

After class,
the girls dance home.
"Watch me!" says Mia.

Mia runs. She leaps.

Oh, no! Ice!

Mia slips and hurts her paw.

# Mia goes to see Dr. Rabbit.

"Sorry, Mia," says Dr. Rabbit.
"No dancing for three weeks."
Mia is very sad.
She will miss the recital!

The next day,

Miss Bird comes to visit.

"I am sorry you cannot dance,"
says Miss Bird.
"But you can still help!"

Mia will be

Miss Bird's special helper!

The next day,
the girls dance.
Mia paints the set.

24

The day after that,
the girls dance.
Mia helps with the lights.

On recital night,

Mia helps Anna with her wings.

Mia helps Ruby tie her shoes.

Mia opens the curtain.

The dancers dance.

What a great recital!

Mia was still a star.

She was a special helper!

Bravo, dancers!

Bravo, Mia!

# Dictionary

## Recital

(you say it like this: ree-sigh-tall)

a special show where dancers perform

## Curtain

(you say it like this: ker-tan)

the cloth that covers the stage
before the dance begins

## Set

decorations on the stage

## Costumes

(you say it like this: kah-stooms)

special clothes that dancers wear for a show